"Can I play with it?"
asked Taj.
"Wait until it's dark,"
said Grandpa.

But Taj didn't want to wait.
He shone his torch
and made the baby jump.
"Stop it," shouted Mum.
"Take that torch away!"

Taj went into the garden.

He made Mr Ali jump.

"Stop it," shouted Mr Ali.

"Take that torch away!"

Taj went into the shed
and shone his torch.
It made Dad jump.
"Stop it," shouted Dad.
"Take that torch away!"

Taj's Torch

by Sue Graves and Mirella Mariani

W
FRANKLIN WATTS
LONDON•SYDNEY

It was Taj's birthday.
Grandpa gave him
a big black torch.
"A torch helps you see
in the dark," he said.

Taj saw Mani the dog.

He shone his torch.

He made Mani jump.

Dad was cross.

"Stop it," shouted Dad.

He took the torch away from Taj.

Taj was sad.

He went inside

to play with

Hema the hamster.

But Hema wasn't there.

"Mum, Hema is missing,"

said Taj.

"We must find him."

Everyone looked for Hema.
Dad and Grandpa looked under
the chairs.

Mum looked under the table

"Listen! Down here!" shouted Taj.

"Hema is under the floor."

Dad looked down but it was too dark to see Hema. "We need your torch, Taj," said Dad.

Taj got his torch.

Taj shone his torch so
Dad could see.
Dad got Hema out.

"Well done, Taj," said Mum.

"A torch helps you see
in the dark," said Taj.

Story trail

Start

Start at the beginning of the story trail. Ask your child to retell the story in their own words, pointing to each picture in turn to recall the sequence of events.

Independent Reading

This series is designed to provide an opportunity for your child to read on their own. These notes are written for you to help your child choose a book and to read it independently.

In school, your child's teacher will often be using reading books which have been banded to support the process of learning to read. Use the book band colour your child is reading in school to help you make a good choice. *Taj's Torch* is a good choice for children reading at Green Band in their classroom to read independently.

The aim of independent reading is to read this book with ease, so that your child enjoys the story and relates it to their own experiences.

About the book

Taj is given a torch, and he loves it – but he keeps shining it in people's faces. Then Hema the hamster goes missing and Taj's torch comes in very useful.

Before reading

Help your child to learn how to make good choices by asking: "Why did you choose this book? Why do you think you will enjoy it?" Look at the cover together and ask: "What do you think the story will be about?" Support your child to think of what they already know about the story context. Read the title aloud and ask: "What do you think Taj will do with his torch in this book?"

Remind your child that they can try to sound out the letters to make a word if they get stuck.

Decide together whether your child will read the story independently or read it aloud to you.

During reading

If reading aloud, support your child if they hesitate or ask for help by telling the word. Remind your child of what they know and what they can do independently.

If reading to themselves, remind your child that they can come and ask for your help if stuck.

After reading

Support comprehension by asking your child to tell you about the story. Use the story trail to encourage your child to retell the story in the right sequence, in their own words.

Help your child think about the messages in the book that go beyond the story and ask: "Do you think Taj will shine his torch in people's faces again? Why/why not?"

Give your child a chance to respond to the story: "Did you have a favourite part? Do you know any stories about pets hiding from their owners?"

Extending learning

Help your child understand the story structure by using the same story context and adding different elements. "Let's make up a new story about something else that Taj is given that he needs to learn to use in the right way. What will Taj be given? When should Taj not use it? When should he?"

In the classroom, your child's teacher may be teaching polysyllabic words (words with more than one syllable). There are many in this book that you could look at with your child, for example: birth/day, un/til, Grand/pa, shout/ed, gar/den, a/way, miss/ing, in/side, ta/ble.

Franklin Watts
First published in Great Britain in 2020
by The Watts Publishing Group

Copyright © The Watts Publishing Group 2020

Series Editors: Jackie Hamley and Melanie Palmer
Series Advisors: Dr Sue Bodman and Glen Franklin
Series Designer: Peter Scoulding

A CIP catalogue record for this book is
available from the British Library.

ISBN 978 1 4451 7076 3 (hbk)
ISBN 978 1 4451 7078 7 (pbk)
ISBN 978 1 4451 7077 0 (library ebook)

Printed in China

Franklin Watts
An imprint of
Hachette Children's Group
Part of The Watts Publishing Group
Carmelite House
50 Victoria Embankment
London EC4Y 0DZ

An Hachette UK Company
www.hachette.co.uk

www.franklinwatts.co.uk

FSC
www.fsc.org
MIX
Paper from
responsible sources
FSC® C104740